Text by Lois Rock
Illustrations copyright © 2014 Kay Widdowson
This edition copyright © 2014 Lion Hudson

Published by Lion Children's Books
an imprint of
Lion Hudson plc
Wilkinson House, Jordan Hill Road,
Oxford OX2 8DR, England
www.lionhudson.com/lionchildrens

ISBN 978 0 7459 6455 3

First edition 2014

A catalogue record for this book is available from the British Library

Printed and bound in China, June 2014, LH17

tiny tots
Christmas

Retold by Lois Rock
Illustrated by Kay Widdowson

LION
CHILDREN'S

Long ago, in Nazareth,
lived a young woman
named Mary.

She was daydreaming
about her wedding…
when the angel
Gabriel appeared.

"Don't be afraid,"
said the angel. "God
has chosen you to do
something very special.

"God wants you to be the mother of his Son,
Jesus. He will bring God's blessing to the
world."

Mary was puzzled, but she believed
everything the angel said.

"I will do as God wants," she agreed.

Joseph was the carpenter in Nazareth. He was looking forward to the day he married Mary.

Then came troubling news: Mary was expecting a baby… and he wasn't the father.

"Whatever shall I do?" he wondered.

In a dream, an angel spoke to him: "Everything that is happening is what God wants," said the angel, "and God wants you to take care of Mary and her child."

"Then so I will," agreed Joseph.

In those days, an emperor named Augustus ruled the land. His messenger arrived in Nazareth.

"Everyone must go to their home town," he cried.

"Everyone must put their names on a list. Then the emperor will know who has to pay taxes."

Joseph made a plan. "My home town is Bethlehem," he said.

"As we are going to be a family, we will go there together!"

They set out on a journey of many miles.

There were lots of other people who were making the journey to Bethlehem. When Mary and Joseph arrived, there was no room left in the inn.

The only place where they could shelter was a stable.

There Mary's baby, Jesus, was born.

While Mary wrapped him in swaddling clothes, Joseph filled a manger with soft straw and blankets.

"This can be the baby's first cradle," he said.

Out on the hillside, shepherds were watching over their sheep.

"I hate these dark nights," said one, "with all the wild animals creeping around to steal sheep."

"It's the daytime that bothers me," said another, "with the emperor's men creeping around to charge us taxes."

"One day," said a third shepherd, "God will send someone to be our king and save us."

Just then, an angel appeared.

"I bring good news," cried the angel. "Tonight, in Bethlehem, a baby has been born.

"He is God's chosen king! He is the one who will save you from all that's wrong.

"You will find him wrapped in swaddling clothes and lying in a manger."

Then all the sky was filled with angels singing:
  Glory to God!
  Peace on Earth!

When the angels had gone, the shepherds hurried to Bethlehem.

They found the stable, with Joseph and Mary, and little baby Jesus.

Mary listened carefully as they told their story about the angels.

All the while, some wise men were making their way to Bethlehem.
   A bright star shone on the road.

"The new star we saw in our own country has guided us all this way," they said.

"We are sure it will lead us to a newborn king."

The star led the men to the place where Mary and Jesus were.
   The wise men brought out their gifts: gold, frankincense, and myrrh.

After the men had gone, Joseph had a dream.
   "Hurry," said an angel. "There is danger here. Take Mary and Jesus far away until it is safe to go back to Nazareth."
   So the little family set out. Joseph and Mary both knew they must take great care of Jesus: so he could grow up safely and bring God's blessing to the world.